Read . . .

along as Handy Bob slings his mop and swabs with pride. Then

Click . . .

into the world of Lakeside School where you can . . .

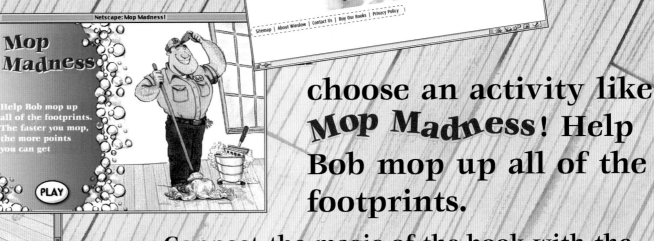

Netscape:Winslow Press: The Feet in the Gym

WINSLOW PRESS

KIDS Teens Parents Teachers Librarians

Books   Jump to a book...   ages 4-9

News Reviews Events

The Feet in the Gym

By Teri Daniels
Illustrated by Travis Foster

Handy Bob needs to keep on his toes at the lively Lakeside gym. He swings his mop and swabs with pride and flings the soapy suds aside. This lovable school custodian is soon at his wit's end, however, as bustling students track dirt, grime, grit and slime across his freshly mopped floor. But help is afoot! Without missing a beat, the children clear the mess with a wild and wonderful solution.

Reviews new!
Signings new!
Author | Illustrator
Book Info

did you know...
Some colleges have more than 900 people in their marching bands.

games
Play Mop Madness!
Help Bob mop up all of the footprints.

links

Sitemap | About Winslow | Contact Us | Buy Our Books | Privacy Policy

Netscape: Mop Madness!

Mop Madness

Help Bob mop up all of the footprints. The faster you mop, the more points you can get

PLAY

Mop Madness!
Score
225

choose an activity like **Mop Madness!** Help Bob mop up all of the footprints.

Connect the magic of the book with the wonder of the Web as you READ AND CLICK at:

winslowhouse.com

LC #: 98-89831
ISBN: 1-890817-12-0 (hardcover); 1-58837-023-2 (paperback)

Creative Director: Bretton Clark
Designer: Billy Kelly

The illustrations in this book were prepared with watercolor and ink.

2 4 6 8 10 9 7 5 3

WinslowHouse

115 East 23rd Street
10th Floor
New York, NY 10010

Printded in China through Palace Press International

Discover *The Feet in the Gym*'s interactive Web site
with worldwide links, games, activities, and more at:

winslowhouse.com

The Feet in the Gym

For my loving family
and the friends and staff of the Norman J. Levy Lakeside School.
Thanks for the inspiration.

T. D.

To Sarah, my beautiful princess, in celebration of our friendship, love and
mutual understanding that it is my job to keep the floors clean.

T. F.

The Feet in the Gym

Teri Daniels

Illustrated by Travis Foster

WinslowHouse

At Lakeside School, I work each day
to wipe each dab of dirt away.
I search for bits of grit and grime,
specks of mud and drops of slime.

I wash the walls and scrape the floors,
shine the knobs and scrub the doors,
dust the lightbulbs when they're dim,
but most of all . . . I mop the gym.

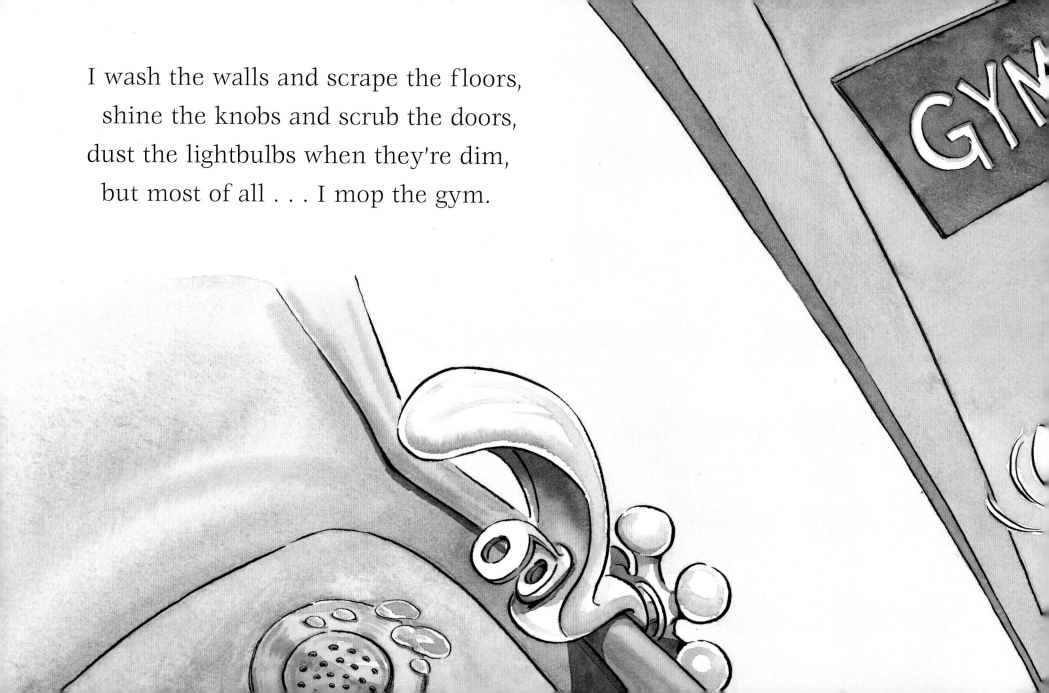

The children call me Handy Bob.
My hands can handle any job.
By far, the hardest job I do
is wiping after every shoe . . .

western boot or wooden clog,
sneaker from a morning jog,
slipper, sandal, soccer cleat—
all the shoes on all the feet!

Without delay, I plop my mop
into my pail filled to the top.
I swab the gym with suds galore
to lift the footprints off the floor.

Every day, I try to beat
  the mass of moving, messing feet.
Before the floor begins to dry,
  the kindergartners shuffle by.

Holding hands, they walk in twos.
I bend down low to count their shoes.
Even though their feet are small,
they leave their footprints, one and all.

I don't like dirty footprint spots.
It's time to peel those polka dots.
I mopped before; I'll mop once more,
until I spy a spotless floor.

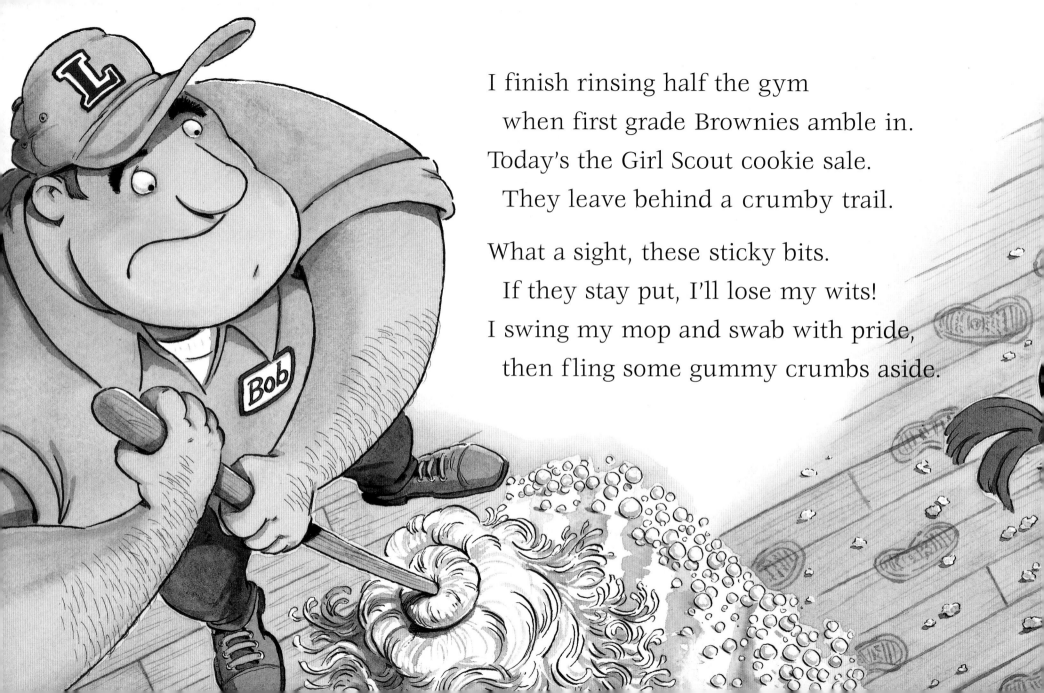

I finish rinsing half the gym
  when first grade Brownies amble in.
Today's the Girl Scout cookie sale.
  They leave behind a crumby trail.

What a sight, these sticky bits.
  If they stay put, I'll lose my wits!
I swing my mop and swab with pride,
  then fling some gummy crumbs aside.

I clear a path that's clean and bright;
then all at once I freeze with fright.
This cannot be! It's just a dream!
Is this the third grade soccer team?

The Lakeside Zappers swiftly pass
and leave a field of tattered grass.
Soccer cleats, the mess they make—
Where's the gardener? Where's the rake?

I douse my mop and start to push
the icky, sticky, grassy mush.
Tip-toe-tap into the goop
goes Mrs. Milton's dancing troupe.

Ballet slippers dip and poke
to dance upon the planks of oak.
They pierce the mushy mess with ease.
Now my floor looks like Swiss cheese!

Art class follows in a rush.
  Paint drips from each painter's brush.
Drops of red and blue and green
  blend into a rainbow scene.

Second graders slide that 'bow,
   arm in arm and toe to toe.
Swirling, curling, skating mates
   sketch a set of figure eights.

Rainbow stains are tough to clear.
   I scrub eight times, then faintly hear . . .
a gentle beat upon a drum,
   a folk guitar, a banjo strum,

a flute, a gong, a saxophone,
  a trumpet and a slide trombone,
a bump, a thump, a pounding sound,
  banging, clanging all around!

When all the noise gets louder still,
the jumping gym begins to fill:
One hundred *feet*, one hundred *hands*,
two romping, stomping Lakeside *bands*!

They sweep the floor and whisk the goo.
  A bit sticks onto every shoe!
Then to the football field they go . . .
  this crowd pleasing, cheese squeezing,
grass raking, mush taking,
  crumb kicking, dot sticking,
merry making music show.

Joy of joys! My lucky day!
  The children marched the mess away!
No need to mop the gym at all.
  The floor is clean from wall to wall.

But wait . . . I do see one small spot,
  one purple-painted polka dot.
It glints and shimmers like a jewel
  upon the gym at Lakeside School.

Round and round the room I glide.
My handy hands reach far and wide.
I blot that dot and scrub that floor.
I need not mop a minute more!

Yes, children call me Handy Bob.

My hands can handle *any* job.

By far the hardest job I do

is wiping after every shoe.